MR.MEN **LITTLE MISS**

MR. MEN and LITTLE MISS™ © THOIP (a Chorion Company)

www.mrmen.com

Mr. Men and Little Miss™ Text and illustrations
© 2010 THOIP (a Chorion company).
Printed and published under licence from
Price Stern Sloan, Inc., Los Angeles.

Original creation by Roger Hargreaves
Illustrated by Adam Hargreaves
First published in Great Britain 1998
This edition published in Great Britain in 2010 by Dean,
an imprint of Egmont UK Limited
239 Kensington High Street, London W8 6SA

Printed in Italy
ISBN 978 0 6035 6571 7

1 3 5 7 9 10 8 6 4 2

LITTLE MISS TINY
JUST THE RIGHT SIZE

Roger Hargreaves

DEAN

Little Miss Tiny lives in a mousehole in the dining-room of Home Farm.

One day she woke up early and decided to go exploring.

Exploring upstairs!

In all the time she had lived at Home Farm she had never been upstairs.

Well, when you are as small as Little Miss Tiny, a staircase is like a mountain.

Little Miss Tiny started to climb the stairs.

She climbed, and she climbed, and she climbed some more.

All the way to the top.

It took her nearly the whole morning!

Everything was very quiet because everyone had gone out for the day.

She wandered through the bedrooms.

She explored the bathroom.

And then she discovered the nursery.

Lying on the floor was a box with a hook on the lid.

She lifted the hook ...

... and got the fright of her life.

"Help!" she shrieked, and hid under the bed.

After a while she plucked up courage and peeked out.

"You silly-billy," she said to herself, "it's only a jack-in-the-box."

She began to look around.

It was wonderful.

She said, "How do you do," to a very serious-looking soldier.

She tickled a teddy bear.

And climbed a tower of blocks.

It was from the top of the blocks
that Little Miss Tiny saw the most
wonderful sight she had seen in all
her tiny life.

A doll's house!

Little Miss Tiny opened the front door and went in.

Everything was just the right size for her. The chairs, the table, the cups and even the stairs.

She went upstairs.

And lay down on the bed and closed her eyes.

She suddenly woke up with a start.

There, looking through the bedroom window of the doll's house, was the farm cat!

Little Miss Tiny didn't know what to do. How was she going to get back to her mousehole?

She went downstairs and through a door.

The farm cat watched her through the windows.

She found herself in a garage on the side of the doll's house, and in the garage was a wind-up toy car.

The little car gave her an idea.

She turned the key on the car, wound it up and jumped in.

The little car took off like a rocket through the little garage doors and straight through the cat's legs!

The car and Little Miss Tiny raced across the carpet, out through the door and down the landing.

Little Miss Tiny laughed with glee.

And then realised she had laughed too soon.

The car shot over the top step of the stairs and out into space and down ...

and down ...

and down ...

Little Miss Tiny shrieked.

With a SPLASH! she landed in the cat's bowl of milk at the bottom of the stairs.

She rushed through the hall, ran across the dining-room floor and back to the safety of her mousehole.

"Phew! That was close!" she said,
with a big sigh of relief.

Well, a big sigh of relief for someone
as tiny as Little Miss Tiny.